BUT IN THE TWENTY-FIRST CENTURY, THE WORLD HAS BECOME MUCH MORE COMPLICATED.

OUR HOMES ARE GUARDED BY BURGLAR ALARMS AND CCTV.

WE BUY FOOD FROM THE SUPERMARKET INSTEAD OF CHASING IT.

WE HAVE SPECIAL HEAT-SEEKING CAMERAS TO FIND MISSING PEOPLE.

HUMAN BEINGS HAVE BECOME A LOT CLEVERER.

SO HAVE DOGS...

This city dog pound may look like an ordinary home for stray dogs, but...

...deep under the pound is something far from ordinary: the secret headquarters of the famous

HEROIC HOUNDS WHOSE PAW-POSE IN LIFE
IS TO SAVE HUMANS IN DISTRESS

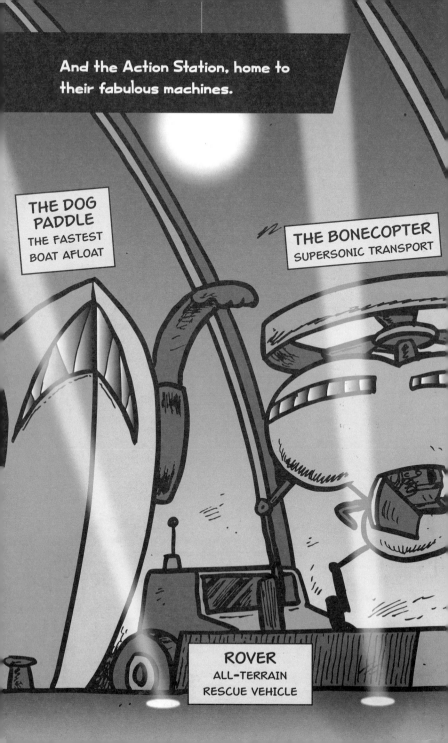

"I'm fed up with lying doggo down here," complained Benji.

Sally sighed. "I know what you mean. It's no fun being an Action Dog if there isn't any action. We haven't been called out to rescue anyone for ages."

"Even our arch-enemy, Katmanchew, has been lying low," said Spike.

Master Yi, the wise old expert in the mystical martial art of Taekwondog, nodded. "Katatonic, he has been."

Benji scratched his ear. "At least Murdoch's had time to finish his new machine. Does anybody know what it is?"

He didn't have long to wait for an answer. Murdoch appeared and stood facing the Action Dogs.

THANKS FOR COMING TO THIS WEE BRIEFING. NOW PAY ATTENTION. THIS IS MY LATEST INVENTION.

Murdoch held up a remote control and pressed a button.

The floor slid back and a brand-new addition to the Action Dogs' fantastic life-saving machines rose from Murdoch's basement workshop.

Rascal gave a low whistle. "This machine is where it's at – dig up a bone in no time flat."

Murdoch glared at him. "I've not been working like a dog on this machine so you can dig up bones, you greedy guts! It's for rescuing people trapped in caves and mines and suchlike."

9

I CALL IT THE DOGGY-DIGGER. THIS WEE BEAUTY WILL TUNNEL THROUGH ANYTHING!

Sally quickly moved to soothe the Scottie's ruffled feelings. "It looks wonderful, Murdoch, I can't wait to see it in action..."

Just then:

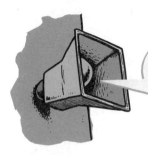

ATTENTION! HEY, GANG. I NEED YOU BACK IN THE POUND RIGHT AWAY. WELFARE OFFICER BRICK JUST CALLED. INSPECTION!

"That's Janet's voice," said Sally. "She's in the Listening Post keeping an ear open for distress messages so Yapper could come to Murdoch's briefing."

Spike called Janet on his dogtooth radio. "Do you want us to bring Yapper's stand-in dummy?"

"*Negative,*" replied Janet. "*I think Brick's planning to take us out somewhere. The dummy will fool him if it's just standing in line, but you can't make it walk!*"

"F.I.D.O." Spike was already heading for the exit. "We need to ditch these uniforms and get up there, pronto. You too, Yapper."

Yapper was horrified. "But we should have someone at the Listening Post 24/7. If Janet's looking after Officer Brick, and he's inspecting us, there'll be nobody there!"

"Can't be helped," growled Spike. "This is an emergency. In any case, we haven't had a distress call for weeks. Let's move it!"

Welfare officer Brick came around the corner with Janet the kennelmaid just as the last of the dogs stepped into line for his inspection.

Brick didn't like dogs, and the dogs in the pound didn't like him.

"You are very lucky dogs," Welfare Officer Brick continued. "Personally, I don't think a bunch of good-for-nothing strays like you deserve special treatment; but I have an invitation for you all to visit an art exhibition!"

Benji groaned aloud. "Art!" he muttered. "I hate art!"

"I love art." Katmanchew, the criminal mastermind who was number one on the Feline Bureau of Investigation (FBI) Most Wanted list, chuckled to himself. "Not to look at – to steal!"

IT SAYS HERE THAT THE VAN DER HUND MUSEUM IS HOLDING A SPECIAL EXHIBITION OF CANINE ART.

Katmanchew's servant Katnip bowed deeply. "I did not think, O great master, that you would be interested in pictures or statues of dogs."

"Oh, but I am, Katnip," growled Katmanchew. "Because if I have those paintings and statues, it means that our enemies do *not* have them. In any case, my spies tell me that they are worth a lot of money – and I am *always* interested in money."

Katmanchew took a deep breath. "Forgive my temper, faithful minion. You do well to remind me of the Action Dogs. But never fear. I have a plan so cunning and vile that, if it succeeds, we will not only steal a stupendous amount of treasure – we will be rid of those mangy interfering mutts for good."

Katnip bowed again. "Truly, master, your evil knows no bounds."

Katmanchew gave a savage grin. "Switch on the hologram viewer. I wish to speak to the special agent I have hired to carry out this fiendish crime: the most glamourpuss spy in the world."

For once, Katnip was startled. "Surely, master, you don't mean..."

"Yes, La Femme Nikitty!" Katmanchew's evil grin grew wider. "Put her on."

Benji looked around the gallery. "I spy with my little eye," he said glumly, "something beginning with P." After a moment, he exclaimed, "Picture! Well done, Benji. I spy with my little eye, something beginning with A.P." Pause. "Another Picture!"

Sally gave him a sideways glance. "You're not enjoying this, are you?"

"It's boring," moaned Benji.

"Cheer up," Sally told him. "Look at this wonderful painting by Salvador Doggi."

"The one with the melting clock? It's rubbish. Chocolate dog-treats melt – clocks don't." Benji looked around at all the well-fed dogs following their owners around the gallery. "Why are there so many dogs here anyway?"

"Cornelius Van Der Hund is the richest man in the world," Sally went on. "He's also a keen collector. This museum of his is full of the world's greatest treasures. He's also crazy about dogs. He thinks dogs are like small furry people."

Benji stared at her. "He thinks dogs are people? That's crazy!"

"That's what I said. Anyway, he's invited us to this special preview of his exhibition – the public don't get to see it until the Grand Opening tonight." Sally gave a gasp. "Oh, look, there he is now!"

"Yes, that's Mr. Van Der Hund," said Sally crossly. "I've seen his picture in magazines. And the dog is his very own pet Chihuahua, Foofoo."

"And she's not soppy-looking!" Yapper had joined them.

I THINK SHE LOOKS REALLY NICE.

"Yapper fancies Foofoo!" chortled Benji. "Yapper fancies Foofoo!"

"Benji!" snapped Sally, "stop teasing. Yapper's already upset because he's had to leave the

Listening Post, and you're just making things worse."

"Well, this is a waste of time," growled Benji. "I want to go back to the pound."

Sally glared at him.

HONESTLY, BENJI! IF YOU'RE GOING TO BE SUCH A DOG IN THE MANGER, I THINK I'LL LOOK AROUND THE REST OF THE EXHIBITION ON MY OWN!

BOTTICOLLIE

Sally stalked away. Both she and Benji were so cross, they didn't notice that they were being watched...

**MUCH ARTISTIC
APPRECIATION LATER**

Sally was in the sculpture hall, looking at busts
of famous composers, when Welfare Officer
Brick came in with a man in uniform.

"Since we were at school together? Ages!" cried Potts.

"You've done well for yourself." Officer Brick gave his old friend an envious look. "Head of Security at the Van Der Hund Museum."

Potts shrugged modestly.

"Well, you know... Here, let me show you round. I'll take you to see the pride of Mr. Van Der Hund's exhibition!"

Sally decided to follow them. This could be interesting.

Officer Brick and his friend strolled through the gallery, past busts of more famous composers – Wolfhound Amadogus Mozart, Poochini, Offenbark – still talking nineteen to the dozen. Sally followed them down a corridor and into a small gallery that contained only one painting.

Welfare Officer Brick rubbed his chin. "It's a bit small, isn't it?"

Potts looked annoyed. "It may be small, but it's priceless."

Brick gave him a sly look. "These paintings must be worth millions! I wouldn't like to be in your shoes if anyone stole them."

Potts laughed. "Impossible! Our security system is foolproof! We've got motion sensors, lasers, infrared, the whole works! Watch..." He reached out towards the painting...

As the guards went out, Brick mopped his brow with a handkerchief. "Whew! I see what you mean. But if no one can get at the paintings, what happens if there's a fire?"

Potts laughed. "No problem. If the fire alarm goes off, the security system shuts down automatically so we can get the paintings out quickly."

Sally had heard enough. She slipped away to find the other Dogs.

Sally looked worried. "No," she said. "Last time I saw him, he wasn't in a good mood. And when Benji's not in a good mood, he gets a bit...reckless. I hope he doesn't do anything silly."

Benji was wandering round the Van Der Hund museum feeling fed up.

There was hardly anyone in the rest of the museum – everyone seemed to be in the Canine Art exhibition. That was fine with Benji. He wanted to be alone. He was sorry he'd annoyed Sally, who was usually nice to him. He knew he'd been rude and sulky and he ought to apologize, but he didn't think there was a dog's chance that Sally would forgive him.

Benji realized he had wandered into a gallery displaying the fossilized skeletons of the biggest dogs that had ever lived: the gigantic *Diplodogus* and the terrifying *Terriersaurus rex*.

A Chihuahua was looking at the skeletons. At first Benji thought it was Yapper. He decided to apologize for his behaviour earlier. He was just about to call out, when...

Benji felt his blood boiling. The cheek of it! A cat, disguised (yeuch!) as a dog, had sneaked into Mr. Van Der Hund's museum – and she was spying for Katmanchew!

Benji didn't hesitate. As the imposter ended the call and put her fake head back on, he sprang into action.

YIKES!

The felonious feline leaped for her life and took shelter inside the ribcage of the *Diplodogus*.

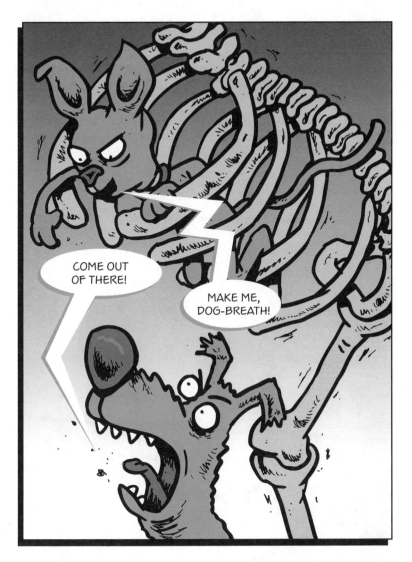

Benji wasn't in the mood to be cheeked by
a mangy moggie, especially one disguised as a
Chihuahua. He looked round for a weapon.

38

Benji lay among the remains and groaned. He was deep in dogosaur doo-doo, and no mistake.

Benji had only just managed to dig himself out from the pile of bones when two burly security men burst into the gallery. They stared at the wreckage in disbelief.

"Cor!" said one.

"Blimey!" said the other.

The first guard pointed at the pile of bones and stared at Benji. "Did you do that?"

"Woof," explained Benji. "Woof, woof. Growl, bark."

The guards didn't look convinced by Benji's explanation. He realized that he wasn't wearing the translator collar the Action Dogs needed to talk to humans. The guards couldn't understand a word he said – but even if they could, he didn't think they would believe that smashing the skeletons had been an accident. The spying cat had disappeared; the only way Benji could prove what had really happened was to find her again.

So when the guards made a grab for him, there was only one thing for it...

Benji raced through galleries, sniffing to left and right. The spy might look like a dog, but she would still smell like a cat.

He finally picked up the scent outside the Arms

and Armour exhibition. He followed it through the gallery, nose to the floor. Then suddenly, in the doorway to the next gallery, he saw...

Benji didn't hesitate. Now he had the spy in sight, he didn't need his nose. He made straight for the feline impostor, teeth bared in a ferocious snarl. The spy took to her heels.

Benji had no time to stop and explain. And when the spy leaped into Mr. Van Der Hund's arms...

The fight didn't last long. Benji, flushed with success, grabbed the spy's fake head to show who she really was. But...

Benji let out a groan as the horrible truth dawned. He had followed the wrong Chihuahua! This wasn't Katmanchew's spy – it was Mr. Van Der Hund's beloved pet!

As the van took them back to the pound, Benji
tried to tell Sally and the others what had really
happened. But they were so angry they wouldn't
listen.

BUT IT'S TRUE! THERE
WAS A SPY!

"Rubbish!" growled Yapper. "You just wanted to
have a fight with Foofoo because she's smaller
than you. You big bully!"

47

"But I didn't—" began Benji.

"I don't think he chased Foofoo becase he's a bully," said Spike.

Benji gave a sigh of relief. "Thanks, Spike."

"I think he chased Foofoo because he's off his rocker."

"Spike!" snapped Sally. She gave Benji a sympathetic look. "Benji, I'm sure you thought you saw a cat, but—"

"I *did* see a cat!" wailed Benji. "Why won't you believe me?"

Spike snorted. "Sure you did! You saw a bad pussycat dressed as a Chihuahua, and you got us thrown out of the museum, and you got Janet in trouble, and you got Welfare Officer Brick really mad at you. You'll be lucky if he doesn't put you in the doghouse for this."

Benji gave Spike a worried look. "I've heard of being 'in the doghouse' when you're in trouble – but that's just an expression." He looked up and realized all the other dogs were looking at him. "Er...isn't it?"

Benji gave a howl of despair. Even Janet was against him!

"And make sure he keeps quiet!" shouted Brick.

Benji heard Janet and Brick go away. For a while, nothing happened. Benji sat down and stared at the wall. He felt more and more miserable and alone. But then he heard a whisper outside his cell. "Psssst!"

Benji put his nose through the bars. His visitor was Rascal.

The spaniel looked around quickly to make sure no one was watching. Keeping his voice low, he said, "Too bad, dude, you took a fall..." He looked round again, then took a baseball and a catcher's mitt from behind his back and passed them to Benji through the bars in the door. "Kill some time by playin' ball."

"Thanks, Rascal," sniffed Benji. At least someone still liked him.

So Benji started killing time...

Later that evening, Spike found Sally lying in her kennel.

"There you are!" he said. "I missed you at chow time. Listen, there are some really brilliant new smells on the widdling post by the main gate. Come and have a sniff."

Spike gave her an angry look. "What's eating you? I know we haven't had a mission lately, and we're all bored, but—"

Sally sighed. "It's not that."

"Oh, I get it," growled Spike. "You're pining over Benji."

"And Janet. Brick sent her home because she wanted to let Benji out for some exercise." Sally's voice was serious. "Listen, Spike, I've been thinking. Suppose Benji really did see a cat disguised as a dog, like he said—"

Spike gave an angry bark. "Don't tell me you're going crazy too—"

But he was interrupted by the wailing of the emergency siren...

ARROUGA! ARROUGA!

IT'S THE ALARM!

As they dropped through the earth, Spike said, "At last! A bit of action! I wonder what the emergency is."

"We'll know soon enough," said Sally. The kennel stopped and she and Spike headed for the Action Station.

They found Murdoch and Rascal already changed into their uniforms and ready for action. Yapper was standing in front of a large TV monitor and holding up a remote control.

"Trouble, gang," he said. "Watch this. I picked it up from the live newsfeed five minutes ago." He pressed a button and the TV screen flickered into life.

HUNDREDS OF GUESTS ATTENDING THE GRAND OPENING OF THE VAN DER HUND MUSEUM WERE EVACUATED FROM THE BURNING BUILDING BEFORE THE FIRE TOOK HOLD. OVER TO OUR REPORTER ON THE SCENE...

GERALD, THEY'RE SAYING HERE THAT THE BLAZE IS TOO BIG FOR THE FIRE DEPARTMENT. THE ONLY ORGANIZATION CAPABLE OF DEALING WITH THIS SORT OF DISASTER IS THE ACTION DOGS...

"This is definitely a job for us," said Spike.

"We'll need the Firedog."

"How will we get it to the fire?" asked Sally.

"With the Bonecopter?"

56

Spike shook his head. "It's only just across town. It'll be quicker to go straight there by road. Let's move!"

"What about Benji?" protested Sally.

"What about him?" Spike shot back. "You heard Brick. He stays locked up."

Sally was dismayed. "But Benji's a member of the team. Anyway, if we don't take him, we'll be a dog short."

"No problem," growled Spike. "Yapper can come."

Yapper beamed. "I can? Really? Oboyoboy!"

Sally followed Spike as he ran to the Firedog and climbed into the driver's seat. "But Brick sent Janet home," she said. "If Yapper comes with us there'll be no one at the Listening Post. What if something goes wrong?"

"Something's already gone wrong," Spike told her. "We're short-pawed because Benji's been grounded for chasing invisible cats. He has to do his time and we have to keep going without him. Now quit yapping, we're in a hurry!" He started the engine. "Hold tight, gang, here we go!"

SMOKE

Sally was speaking into her dogtooth radio as Spike stopped the Firedog outside the museum. "Action Dogs to Fire Department – hey, guys. Can you give us a heads-up on what's happening out there?" She listened intently for a moment, then reported, "They're pulling back. They've tried pouring water on the flames and it's had no effect."

"Water!" growled Murdoch in a disgusted voice. "No use at all! The Firedog's belly tanks are full of my special foam. We'll need maximum clearance for the sprayer – prepare to raise leg!"

Spike reached for the controls. "F.I.D.O."

Spike gave Murdoch an angry look. "Your so-called special foam is a washout! It's not even touching the flames."

"That's impossible!" Murdoch snapped back. "That foam could put out a volcano!" He rubbed his chin thoughtfully. "There's something mighty fishy going on here..."

SPIKE, ALL THOSE PRICELESS TREASURES WILL BE BURNED TO ASHES – WE HAVE TO DO SOMETHING.

SHUT UP AND LET ME THINK.

Rascal shook his head. "Thinking time's what we ain't got. I say strike while the iron is hot."

"Maybe we should send someone back for the Doggy-digger," said Spike. "Then we could tunnel down under the flames. What do you think, Murdoch... Murdoch?" He gave an angry growl. "Where is he?"

Sally looked out of the door and her eyes opened wide in horror.

THERE HE IS!

Spike, Sally, Yapper and Rascal hurried down to the street – but Murdoch had nearly reached the fire.

"He's gone crazy!" whined Yapper.

Rascal bit his claws. "What's the matter with the dude? He's fixin' to get barbecued!"

Sally was horrified. "We've got to stop him."

Spike shook his head. "It's too late – there's nothing we can do!"

They gazed in horror at the wall of flame through which their companion had disappeared.

"Murdoch!" yelped Sally.

"Don't waste your breath," Spike told her gruffly. "That suit won't protect him in a fire like this. He's a goner."

Tears shone in Sally's eyes. "Oh, Murdoch!"

Yapper's ears drooped; then they perked up again. "No – wait. Look!"

Rascal whistled. "Awesome, dawg, and that's no joke. Thought you'd just gone up in smoke!"

Sally gave a cry of relief. "Oh, thank goodness! The suit protected him after all."

Murdoch gave her a glare. "The suit had nothing to do with it!" He stripped off one of his gloves and stuck his paw into the flames. The others gasped in horror, but when Murdoch pulled his paw out again it wasn't even singed.

"I knew there was something fishy when my foam didn't work," he growled. "These flames look hot, but they aren't. That's because they're not real – they're holograms. Just projected 3D images."

His friends gaped with astonishment and Murdoch sighed. "Don't you get it, yet? This whole thing is a fake. There is no fire!"

"Ze fake flames are very convincing," continued Nikitty. "Ze police and fire department purrrceive ze fire to be real. Zey 'ave evacuated ze museum, zey will not go back into it until ze fire is out, and zey are keeping ze public well back from ze building."

"Excellent!" Katmanchew rubbed his paws. "And the Action Dogs?"

"Zey have stopped trying to put out ze fire. I think purrrhaps zey suspect ze truth. Do I have purrrmission to proceed?"

"Yes!" hissed Katmanchew. "Go to Phase Three."

As the figure of Nikitty faded, the criminal mastermind turned to his loyal servant. His eyes glowed with wickedness.

"You see, Katnip?" he gloated. "My plan is working. Soon, those do-gooding dogs will fall into my trap. And after that, they will never trouble me again."

Katnip bowed low. "Master, you will make cats' paws of your enemies. Truly, you are the cat's pyjamas."

Katmanchew smirked. "I know."

Spike shook his head in bafflement. "I don't get it. Who would pull a stunt like this?"

"Katmanchew!" said Murdoch. "Who else?"

"But why?"

"I know why," said Sally. "When the fire alarm goes off, it shuts down all the burglar alarms in the museum. I heard their security man telling Welfare Officer Brick about it this morning."

Murdoch nodded slowly. "And with the alarms turned off, Katmanchew's gang can just walk in and take anything they like."

"Then we have to get the alarms turned back on!" said Spike. "Where are they?"

Sally frowned. "The security man said something about the basement."

"Come on then!" said Spike.

70

Spike led the way into the museum and along the main corridor to the Canine Art gallery. He looked around the empty room.

"Well, the art collection is still here," he said firmly.

IN ANY CASE, OUR FIRST JOB IS TO MAKE SURE EVERYONE GOT OUT SAFELY. SALLY, YAPPER, MAKE SURE THERE'S NO ONE LEFT INSIDE THE MUSEUM. MURDOCH, RASCAL, YOU'RE WITH ME. LET'S FIND THE ALARM SYSTEM.

He led the way to the service stairs, heading for the basement.

It took Sally and Yapper some time to check that the museum was deserted. But at last they had looked in every gallery.

Sally was puzzled. "It looks as if there's no one here. If the whole fire is a diversion to let

Katmanchew's gang steal all the paintings...where are they?"

Before Yapper could reply, a faint voice behind them called, "Help!"

Sally caught the fainting Chihuahua as she fell. "What is it?" she cried.

Foofoo's eyelids flickered. "Mr. Van Der Hund. He's hurt...he needs help...follow me..."

Sally and Yapper quickly followed Foofoo down the service stairs to the basement. They found themselves outside a huge open steel door. Foofoo pointed. "In there..."

Yapper ran for the door. Sally hesitated; she had no idea what was behind the door and wanted to ask Foofoo more questions, but she couldn't let Yapper go off on his own. "Stay there," she told Foofoo. She followed Yapper through the door...

Spike turned to Sally. "I thought you were checking
there was no one left inside the museum."

"We checked," Sally told him, "but then Foofoo
turned up and said Mr. Van Der Hund was hurt..."

"But it wasn't Foofoo!" wailed Yapper.

Rascal shook his head. "Weren't no dog. How
'bout that? Just a bad ol' pussy cat."

"It proves something else as well," said Sally. "It proves that when Benji said he was chasing a cat disguised as a dog, he was telling the truth."

Spike nodded slowly. "I guess that's right. Nikitty must have been spying out the layout of the museum when Benji spotted her."

Sally clenched her paws. "And I'll bet, right now, Nikitty and Katmanchew's gang are helping themselves to all the treasures of the museum."

"We have to stop them!" growled Spike. "I'll call up the Listening Post..." His eyes fell on Yapper. "Oh..."

THERE'S NOBODY AT THE LISTENING POST. YAPPER IS HERE, BENJI'S IN THE DOGHOUSE, JANET'S AT HOME AND MASTER YI WILL BE IN THE DOGJO, MEDITATING.

AND WE NEED BENJI AND MASTER YI HERE NOW. WE'RE IN A REAL JAM!

"It's worse than you think," said Murdoch. "I've been checking out the systems here. We can't reset the alarms until the fire department gives the all-clear – and they still don't know the fire is a fake or they'd be in here by now."

Spike groaned. "So we can't stop Katmanchew's gang."

"And there's more," Murdoch went on. He pointed to a computer screen. "Look at the plans of the building. This isn't just a basement we're in – it's like a bank vault. The walls are a metre thick and that door is bombproof."

"That's bad," said Sally.

"And it's on a time lock, so even if someone out there knew we were in here, they wouldn't be able to open the door for twelve hours."

Sally groaned. "That's really bad."

"Aye," said Murdoch gloomily, "and I haven't even told you the worst of it yet..."

THIS IS WHERE THE MUSEUM KEEPS ALL THE TREASURES THAT ARE TOO OLD AND FRAGILE TO GO ON DISPLAY.

"Oh well," said Sally, trying to sound cheerful, "at least Katmanchew's gang won't be able to steal the stuff down here."

"No," said Murdoch. "But the problem is, you

know how old and fragile things have to be protected from damp and suchlike? Well, that's why, once that door is shut, all the air is pumped out of this basement."

Spike gave him a horrified look. "What are you saying?"

Yapper gave a howl of despair. "It's my fault we're in this mess! If I hadn't dragged Sally in here to save Foofoo's master, we wouldn't all be trapped."

"If I hadn't brought you with us," Spike told him glumly, "we'd still have someone at the Listening Post. It's my fault."

"It doesn't matter whose fault it is," said Sally. "The question is, how do we get out of here?"

Rascal shook his head. "Out, you say? Ain't no way. Looks as though we're here to stay."

"Rascal's right," said Murdoch. "Our radios are useless if there's no one to take our calls."

"That's true," said Sally thoughtfully, "but maybe there's another way."

Spike stared at her. "What do you mean?"

"I mean, we dogs have had ways of talking to each other over great distances before humans invented telephones and radio."

Murdoch fixed her with a beady eye. "Are you

talking about...the Night Howl?"

Sally nodded. "That's exactly what I'm talking about. All dogs know that we can hear each other's voices in the dead of night."

"Primitive, unscientific nonsense!" grumbled Murdoch.

MURDOCH, WE ALL KNOW HOW WONDERFUL YOUR INVENTIONS ARE. BUT SOMETIMES, EVEN SCIENCE CAN'T HELP, AND WE HAVE TO LOOK BACK TO THE OLD WAYS.

Murdoch *hrummph*ed. "There may be something in what you say. But we're a long way underground."

Sally nodded. "I know. But if we all howl together, we might get through..."

"To Benji?" Spike shook his head. "No good. Benji's locked up. Even if he heard the Howl, he couldn't do anything."

"I know Benji's locked up," said Sally. "But Master Yi isn't. And he'll be meditating. If anyone can hear us Howl, he can."

Spike thought about this, and grinned. "All right. It's got to be worth a try. Come on, gang. Let's get into a huddle... Here we go. After three. One...two...three..."

"So the Action Dogs are trapped in the vault?" purred Katmanchew.

"Yes," said Nikitty. "And ze air is running out."

"Can you hear them?"

"No, ze door is too thick – but zere is a video link from inside the vault. I shall opurrrate ze camera..."

Katmanchew chuckled. "*Music to my ears!*"

Nikitty winced. "If you say so. Purrrsonally, I find ze howling of dogs gives me a terrible pain in ze *derrière*."

"*But that sound is not just the howling of dogs – it is the terrified moans of our enemies as they realize that nothing can save them now. Soon, they will be gone for ever – and I, Katmanchew, will have triumphed!*"

"It's not working!" growled Murdoch. "They can't
hear us."

"We're just out of practice," said Sally. "We're so
used to our radios, it's a long time since any of us
have done the Night Howl. We'll get through
eventually. Trust me. Come on, everyone – again."

A few minutes later...

Benji staggered to the door and looked out.
There was no one in sight.

A voice said, "Down here, I am."

Benji looked down. "Master Yi," he yapped.
"What are you doing here?"

Benji gaped at Master Yi. "But that door was locked!"

The old Pekingese shook his head. "In your mind, the door was locked."

"No," said Benji, "it was really locked, with a key and everything!" He stared at Master Yi in awe. "Did you open it with your incredible mental powers?" he breathed. "Did you use strange unknown forces to make the lock think that it *wasn't* locked?"

Master Yi looked puzzled. "No, I opened it with a
Taekwondog flying drop-kick..." He demonstrated
on the wall.

Master Yi tutted. "Time, we are wasting. To the Listening Post with me, you must come." The Master of Taekwondog hurried from the doghouse.

Benji grabbed his baseball and ran to keep up. "Master Yi, you said Sally and the others were in trouble."

"Indeed," snapped Master Yi. "By the Night Howl, contacted me they have. In danger, they are. Unless you can help them, cooked their goose is..."

Before Benji and Master Yi had reached the Listening Post, they could hear Murdoch's voice...

Benji switched the radio to *TRANSMIT*.
"Murdoch, I'm here. Master Yi said you were all in trouble."

"Aye, we are that." Murdoch explained the situation at the museum in a few words. "So ye see, laddie," he concluded, "you're the only one who can help us. Now listen carefully. You'll have to bring the Doggy-digger to tunnel down to us. It's all loaded up in the Bonecopter, so all you have to do is fly it over here. All right?"

Benji nodded solemnly. "I know exactly what you want me to do. It's a terrific plan. There's only one itsy-bitsy, teensy-weensy little problem..."

I CAN'T FLY!

THIS IS A REALLY, REALLY BAD IDEA.

Sally's voice sounded in his earphones. *"Calm down, Benji. We've been through all this. You've watched me fly the Bonecopter."*

"I've watched a cat climb a tree – it doesn't mean *I* can do it!"

"I'm sorry, Benji." Sally's voice was soothing. *"I wouldn't ask you to do this if there was any other way. But we need the Doggy-digger. And you can't tunnel all the way over here, it would take too long."*

98

"I know," moaned Benji.

"All right. Now remember, I'll be telling you what to do every step of the way. Just relax."

"That's easy for you to say!"

Sally ignored this. *"Now, the first thing you have to do is switch on the smoke machines so nobody sees the Bonecopter take off."*

"All right," said Benji glumly.

"Benji!" Sally's voice was sharp with worry. *"This is no time to panic!"*

"I'm trying to fly hundreds of tons of complicated machinery," screamed Benji, "and I haven't a clue what I'm doing. I think this is a *terrific* time to panic!"

Just then, something like a cartoon dog lead appeared on the computer screen in front of Benji. A message appeared on the screen:

IT LOOKS LIKE YOU ARE TRYING TO FLY THE BONECOPTER. WOULD YOU LIKE HELP WITH THAT?

Benji screamed, *"Yeeesssss!"*

A moment later, the Bonecopter stopped bouncing all over the sky like a bucking bronco, and levelled off. The shrill whine of the engines settled to a comforting roar.

"Benji! Benji!" Sally's voice was frantic. *"Are you all right?"*

"Yes," gasped Benji. "I think I found the autopilot."

"*Thank goodness for that! I was going to tell you about that before you panicked. Tell it to take the Bonecopter to the Van Der Hund Museum.*"

Benji did so. As the Bonecopter turned onto its new course, he sat back and mopped his brow. "I thought we were goners there."

Master Yi said calmly, "What will be, will be..."

YOU'RE DOING FINE, BENJI.

Rascal panted, "Doing great, but don't be late – we're fixin' to asphyxiate..."

"Aye," growled Murdoch, "if he doesn't get here soon, tell him he needn't bother."

"Give Benji a break, Murdoch," said Sally crossly. "He's doing the best he can..."

"'Ello, fleabags!"

The Dogs looked round, startled. The new voice was coming from a loudspeaker to one side of the door. There was a computer screen with a camera alongside it. Spike switched on the screen and Nikitty appeared.

The feline fraud chuckled. *"I 'ope you are all purrrfectly comfortable."*

Benji and Master Yi climbed into the Doggy-digger's control cabin and strapped themselves in.

The radio crackled. *"Have ye switched on the ground radar to help ye avoid underground obstacles?"* asked Murdoch.

"Of course!" Benji switched off his microphone and hissed at Master Yi, "Where's the switch for the ground radar?"

The old Pekingese shrugged. "A clue, I have not."

"Oh well, I guess we'll manage without it." Benji switched his mic back on. "Ready to start tunnelling."

"All right, Benji." Sally's face replaced Murdoch's on the screen. *"Only...don't take too long, please?"*

THE AIR'S GETTING... A LITTLE THIN DOWN HERE.

After a while, the rumble of the motors rose to a whine. Benji gave Master Yi a worried look. "That means we've hit something really hard, doesn't it? But it can't be the basement wall, not yet..."

"Whoops!" Benji gripped the controls hard. "Sorry about the mess – coming through – watch your backs – please mind the gap between the platform and the big scrabbly thing..."

Master Yi was looking out of a side window. "Worry you, I do not like to: but a train coming is."

In the basement, time was running out.

CAN'T...LAST...MUCH...LONGER.

Spike gritted his teeth in a snarl. "It really burns me up that we can't do anything to stop Nikitty."

Sally reached out and took his paw. "My eyes," she whispered. "It's getting dark... Why is it getting dark?"

"Oops – that was me." Murdoch sounded embarrassed. "The lights in here are on a dimmer switch. I was just messing about...sorry."

Rascal slipped down in his chair. "Air all gone... start to choke... Guess we're all about to croak..."

Very faintly, Yapper said, "Foofoo..."

Spike coughed. "I guess this is it. Goodbye, everyone. You've been a great team..."

But then...

The black-hearted bandit was so busy gloating over her haul that she didn't even notice the rumbling noises coming from under the floor, until...

Spike and Benji led the charge, snatching up dogosaurus bones to use as clubs. Rascal, Sally and the others followed. And very soon...

Benji followed the fleeing feline into the next gallery – but Nikitty was fast. He soon realized he would never catch up with her.

Then he felt a pain under his ribs. *Oh no*, he thought, *what a time to get a stitch!* But as his paw went to his side, Benji felt something round in the pocket of his uniform. His baseball – the one Rascal had given him, the one he had been playing with all day in the doghouse.

Benji took the ball from his pocket and wound up for a perfect pitch...

It took some time for Murdoch to find the hologram generator that was projecting the fake fire, and shut it down. It took even longer to explain to the police and fire department what had really happened at the museum. But eventually, the museum workers were allowed back in to start putting all the stolen treasures back where they belonged.

Mr. Van Der Hund was very relieved that his treasures hadn't gone up in smoke.

Benji was furious! He'd been right all along, and he'd saved his friends – was that all the thanks he was going to get? Just then he noticed that Foofoo was looking in his direction – and...

As Mr. Van Der Hund and Yapper set off in pursuit of Foofoo, two burly policemen came by with Nikitty. Katmanchew's spy was in handcuffs.

Benji held out his baseball. "You'll be needing this," he said. "You're going to have a lot of time to kill in prison."

Nikitty snarled at him. "Keep your stupid, smelly ball, you meddling mutt! I shall spend my time in jail purrrlanning purrrfectly purrrverse ways to get my revenge on you!"

Benji stared at Sally. *"What?"*

"Sorry, Benji," said Sally, "we have to get you back under lock and key before Brick makes his rounds in the morning, or Janet will be in big trouble."

Benji gave her a hangdog look. "I get locked up again? Oh, great!"

Spike came over. "Hey, group, listen up. Before Mr. Van Der Hund skipped out, he told me he's so grateful to the Action Dogs that he's planning to throw a party here at the museum for all the dogs who came to the preview this afternoon." He caught Benji's eye. "Um...apart from Benji, of course."

Benji clenched his paws. "That's so unfair!"

"Don't worry, Benji." Sally rummaged in the bag at her feet. "We'll get you into the party – in disguise."

Benji stared at her. "In disguise as what?"

Sally held up Nikitty's Chihuahua disguise. "Foofoo!"

Katmanchew sat watching one of his many tv screens.

Katmanchew sat back on his throne. "So," he hissed. "Nikitty has failed me."

Katnip bowed low. "So it would appear, master."

Katmanchew's claws left deep grooves in the arms of his throne. "The Action Dogs have interfered with my plans yet again. But I have other evil schemes in hand – so many evil schemes – and next time..."

NEXT TIME:

WILL THE

ACTION DOGS

SURVIVE...

DANGER ON THE ICE

A sudden katastrophic rise in temperature at the South Pole has caused ice sheets to break up, stranding a team of scientists. Only one feline felon could be to blame...

Aboard the Sea Dog, it's full steam ahead for the Action Dogs to save the day. But with sea levels rising, and Katmanchew up to his old tricks, will the Action Dogs sink or swim...?

ISBN 9781409520337

COMING SOON!

OCEAN OF PERIL

When the cruise liner *Dontpanic* is hijacked by ferocious feline Captain Claw, the race is on to stop it crashing into an island full of holidaymakers – and causing a huge nuclear explosion. Can the Action Dogs' newest member Benji prove he's no dogsbody by stopping the ship... Or will they all end up as cat food?

ISBN 9781409520191

OUT NOW!

TERROR IN SPACE

The conniving Katmanchew has set a spaceship on a collision course with a brand-new Space Hotel full of super-rich celebrities. It's time for the Action Dogs to blast off to the rescue in the Dog Starship! But Welfare Officer Brick is inspecting the pound – so it looks like the Action Dogs are firmly grounded.

Can the Dogs escape in time to stop a cosmic katastrophe, or will it all blow up in their faces...?

ISBN 9781409520344

COMING SOON!

BITE (attack factor)	?
BARK (fear factor)	?
SPEED	?
RESCUE CAPABILITY	?

DOGGY-DIGGER

can dig a hole faster than a hundred dogs put together

NIKITTY

the feline spy who's a mistress of disguise

BITE (attack factor)	68
BARK (fear factor)	35
SPEED	
RESCUE CAPABILITY	-10

SALLY

keeps the Action Dogs boys on a tight leash

...ck factor)	80
...factor)	62
	39
...PABILITY	70

MASTER YI

Taekwondog master

HOW TO DRAW YOUR VERY OWN ACTION DOGS...
BY
MARTIN CHATTERTON

1. I like drawing Murdoch most. I start by drawing a circle for the lower part of his head. I add a little rectangular block for the rest of his head and another bigger one for his body. Then I roughly sketch out his arms and legs like this...

2. The next thing I do is add a bit more detail. I put his nose and whiskers on first. Then I add his ears on top of the "block". His eyes are different sizes and he almost always looks grumpy. I'll then add in his paws.

3. Once I've got Murdoch sketched out I'll start putting in all the "tickly" bits – the details. Things like his uniform and all the shading on his fur.

4. The only thing left to do is to add in some greys (or colour if you're planning on doing a colour version). And that's how you draw an Action Dog!

Ta-dah!
You've just learned how to draw Murdoch.

Now why not try some more...

Can you draw Yapper?

1. Sketch the basic shapes...

2. Complete the outline...

3. Add in the detail...

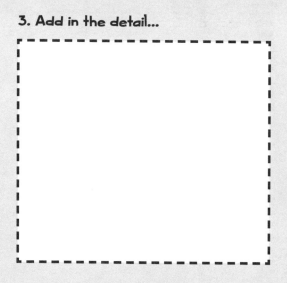

4. And here's how he should look now!

You could even try creating your
own character...

And don't forget to scan in your
pictures and upload them to the
Action Dogs website!

www.actiondogsonline.com

Happy drawing!

FOR MORE FUN READS THAN
YOU CAN SHAKE A CAT AT,
CHECK OUT

www.fiction.usborne.com

Find out more about the 2 Steves at
WWW.THE2STEVES.NET

First published in the UK in 2012 by Usborne Publishing Ltd., Usborne House,
83-85 Saffron Hill, London EC1N 8RT, England. www.usborne.com

Text copyright © Steve Barlow and Steve Skidmore
The right of Steve Barlow and Steve Skidmore to be identified as the authors of this
work has been asserted by them in accordance with the Copyright, Designs and
Patents Act, 1988.

Illustrations copyright © Usborne Publishing Ltd., 2012
Illustrations by Martin Chatterton.

The name Usborne and the devices ♀ ☺ are Trade Marks of
Usborne Publishing Ltd.

This is a work of fiction. The characters, incidents, and dialogues are products of the
author's imagination and are not to be construed as real. Any resemblance to actual
events or persons, living or dead, is entirely coincidental.

A CIP catalogue record for this book is available from the British Library.

ISBN 9781409520320 JF AMJJASOND/12 00489/1
Printed in Dongguan, Guangdong, China.